Dear
Hound

This book
belongs to

_____

Jill Murphy

Dear Hound

Walker & Company 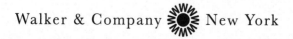 New York

Originally published in Great Britain by Puffin Books, the Penguin Group, in 2009
First published in the United States of America in September 2010 by
Walker Publishing Company, Inc., a division of Bloomsbury Publishing, Inc.
www.bloomsburykids.com

For information about permission to reproduce selections from this book, write to
Permissions, Walker BFYR, 175 Fifth Avenue, New York, New York 10010

Library of Congress Cataloging-in-Publication Data
Murphy, Jill.
Dear hound / Jill Murphy.
p.   cm.
Summary: When Alfie, a timid deerhound puppy, gets lost in the woods, he will do almost
anything—including befriending a pair of foxes—to find his way home to his beloved boy,
Charlie, who refuses to believe Alfie is gone for good.
ISBN 978-0-8027-2190-7
[1. Lost and found possessions—Fiction. 2. Survival—Fiction. 3. Scottish deerhound—
Fiction. 4. Dogs—Fiction. 5. Animals—Infancy—Fiction. 6. Foxes—Fiction.] I. Title.
PZ7.M9534De 2010   [Fic]—dc22   2010006833

Printed in the U.S.A. by Worldcolor Fairfield, Pennsylvania
1 3 5 7 9 10 8 6 4 2

For dear
Sue King
from all our
dear hounds

Dear
Hound

DEERHOUND DETAILS

There are a few things you should know about deerhounds before you read this story about Alfie.

1. EARSTYLES
They have the most expressive ears in the dog world. See the picture "Deerhound Earstyles."

2. SPEED
They can outrun a car at speeds of up to forty miles per hour.

3. DEAR HOUNDS
They are the sweetest, most gentle of hounds, always anxious not to offend their owners.

4. FOOD
Their favorite dinner is beef and their favorite snack is cheese—any type, the smellier the better. They can detect someone opening a bag of potato chips two doors away!

5. NOSE PERISCOPE
They can bend the tips of their noses around a corner.

6. SMILER
Some of them smile when pleased to see you.

7. NEAT EARS
Deerhounds are supposed to have the outer layer of gray fur stripped from the ears, revealing the soft, short black hair beneath.

8. LEANING

They like to lean on people—especially people they love.

9. GARDENING

They are great hole-diggers. Once they've started a hole, they don't stop till Australia.

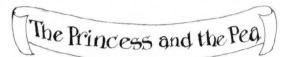

FAVORITE DEERHOUND FAIRY TALE

10. COUCH POTATOES

They are comfort freaks. Only a sofa or bed will do—see picture "Favorite Deerhound Fairy Tale."

11. THE SERPENTINE GROVEL

When especially pleased to see you, or anxious that they've done something wrong, they go into a serpentine grovel, almost tying themselves in a knot. They sometimes twist their head so far toward their tail that they overbalance and fall over.

CHAPTER ONE

It was the start of a perfect autumn day. The sort of day that called you to be up and outside. The sort of day when only good things should happen.

Two cats were hunched on top of the garden wall between their houses. One was a brown-and-cream Ragdoll cat named Florence, and the other was a black-and-white "no particular breed" named Humbug. Both cats sat perfectly still, faces turned to the rising sun, their fur ruffling in the gentle breeze.

"How's it going with the monster?" asked Humbug.

"Better," said Florence, blinking her swimming-pool-blue eyes. "I had a chat with him last week—made a sort of bargain—and now he's a changed dog. Just as well, really. It was beginning to drive me nuts, all that noise and chasing me around the yard."

"How did you do it?" asked Humbug, intrigued. "I can't imagine what bargain you could possibly make with a deerhound."

"It was very easy, actually," explained Florence. "He's scared of thunder, and I mean *really* scared, so I promised I'd always snuggle up with him in the kitchen when there's a storm if he promised never to chase me ever again—or anyone else for that matter—and it worked like magic."

"Cool," said Humbug admiringly.

The sun had made its way up above the roofs and treetops and the two cats heard the first people getting into their cars and going off to work. Florence stood up and stretched herself thoroughly. "I think I'll go home for some breakfast," she said.

"Hope it's something nice," said Humbug.

"It's always the same dried stuff," called Florence over her shoulder. "But it *is* nice. See you around."

"Mmm," purred Humbug.

CHAPTER TWO

In the kitchen, Alfie the deerhound puppy was curled up in a tight ball, fast asleep on an enormous, squishy beanbag. He was in the middle of a delightful dream in which he had just chased Florence to the top of a very bendy tree at the end of the yard. Alfie was standing on his hind legs and pushing the tree with his front paws so that Florence was beginning to lose her grip among the sparse branches.

"Surrender!" barked Alfie.

"Never!" yowled Florence.

The cat-flap banged as Florence arrived in search of her breakfast, and Alfie awoke with a start. For a moment he forgot his bargain and scrambled off the beanbag, barking wildly and sliding around on the tiled floor. Florence jumped up onto the nearest counter.

"Steady, kiddo," she said sternly. "Haven't you heard the weather forecast? We're in for a freak storm over the next couple of days. We made a deal, remember?"

Alfie remembered and slunk back to his beanbag, ears flopped over his forehead in embarrassment.

"Sorry, Florence," he mumbled. "I was dreaming. I only forgot for one moment. I won't do it again, I promise."

"That's all right," said Florence huffily. "I'll let you off *this* time. What happened to your ears?"

Alfie looked puzzled for a second.

"One's smooth and black," explained Florence, "and the other one's hairy and gray like it usually is."

"Oh, *that*," mumbled Alfie. "Well, deerhounds are supposed to have trimmed ears so you can see the black fur underneath. Charlie said it shows you're a grown-up dog when you have your smooth ears done, but it hurt and I only lasted for one ear so they gave up—anyway, no one'll notice."

"*I* noticed," said Florence, "and it looks truly bizarre. Oh well, never mind. Move over and I'll cuddle up with you to keep warm. It's chilly in here with all these tiles and they might not be up for a while."

CHAPTER THREE

Upstairs, Alfie's young master, Charlie, was asleep, dreaming of scoring the perfect goal in a soccer game with all the best players in school. In the dream, Charlie pulled his shirt over his head and ran around the field shouting and yelling for joy, other players grabbing him and thumping him on the back.

"Charlie! Char*lie*!" His mom's voice blasted him awake. "You're all tangled up in your sheets! What on earth were you dreaming about? Come on, we overslept."

Charlie pushed himself up on one elbow

and laughed. "Gosh, Mom," he said ruefully, "that was *some* dream. I wish it were true."

"No time for dreaming!" said his mom. "We have a lot to do. There's breakfast for all of us, then we're off to your cousin Chloe's wedding, so we'd better get a move on."

Charlie groaned. "Oh, Mom," he said. "I wish we didn't have to go."

They padded downstairs together.

"I know," said his mom. "It's such a gorgeous day and I'm not crazy about going *anywhere* except out with Alfie, but I'm sure it'll be fine when we get there—oh, look!"

They had opened the kitchen door, revealing Alfie and Florence curled up together on the beanbag, looking like a picture on a greeting card.

"I *knew* they'd get along in the end." Charlie beamed, plonking himself down on the edge of the beanbag and waking them up with a hug.

"Hey, whoa, Alf! And you, Floss!" He

laughed as Alfie started madly licking his young master's face while Florence leapt into Charlie's arms and was head-butting him under his chin.

CHAPTER FOUR

"**A**re you *sure* Alfie's going to be all right with this lady you found?" asked Charlie through a mouthful of toast.

"Absolutely," said his mom reassuringly. "Her name is Jenny. I answered her ad in the local paper and she sounded *so* nice. I even went to look at the setup, just to make sure. She's been watching other people's dogs for years. She has a dear little house— with a walled backyard and two huge sofas for the dogs to sleep on—oh, and there's a huge field next to a nearby farm with a high hedge and a big gate to keep the dogs safe when they're out walking. So you see, it's perfect. It'll be like a vacation for our dear deerhound. In fact, she'll be here in ten minutes, so we need to hurry."

"How come there's a farm?" asked Charlie. "There aren't usually any farms in a city."

"It's on the *outskirts* of the city," explained his mom, "where the houses meet the countryside, next to Hawkland Woods— we used to go there sometimes when you were little."

The doorbell rang.

"That's her!" said Charlie's mom. "Run and let her in. I'll keep Alfie in here so he doesn't send her flying."

Jenny *was* nice, and amazing with Alfie. Everyone chased each other around the backyard and Alfie was thrilled to find that their visitor had a pocket full of his favorite dog biscuits. He *wasn't* so thrilled when she put him on a leash and set off with him down the path to the van. He splayed out his paws like a donkey and turned his head back toward Charlie, yelping and barking like a demented sea lion.

"Perhaps you both should come out to the van," suggested Jenny. "He'll follow along if he thinks you're coming too."

Charlie and his mom hurried down the path, lugging Alfie's beanbag between them.

They opened the van door and laid the beanbag inside.

"Come on, Alf," coaxed Charlie, perching on the back step of the van and patting the beanbag. "Hop in."

Unable to resist a comfy bed, especially his own, Alfie sprang nimbly over Charlie's knees and into the van, then curled up on the beanbag. Quick as a flash, Charlie jumped up and Jenny slammed the door.

Heartrending howls and yelps started up immediately.

"Don't worry," Jenny shouted, trying to make herself heard above the noise. "He'll be fine once we get back to my place—they always are."

"LET ME OUT!" barked Alfie. "PLEASE LET ME OUT! I'M SORRY I CHASED THE CAT! I'M SORRY I STOLE THE SANDWICHES!"

"Oh, Mom," said Charlie anxiously as Jenny got into the driver's seat. "He *really* doesn't want to go."

Jenny laughed. "Stop worrying," she said soothingly. "He'll have a wonderful time."

"NO I WON'T!" Alfie was barking himself hoarse. "*I'm sorry I ate your mom's handbag! I'm sorry I dug up all the flowers last week—I'll never do it again!* Please *let me out. Please don't send me away! Pleeeeeease!*"

Charlie and his mom held on to each other as they watched the van drive off. They could still hear the desperate howling two streets away.

"I didn't know he'd make such a fuss," said Charlie. "He's so upset."

"Not as upset as Florence," said Charlie's mom, laughing. "Look!"

Florence was strutting indignantly around the kitchen, looking for the beanbag.

Charlie's mom closed the front door and shooed Charlie upstairs.

"He'll only be there for one night," she said, trying to sound cheerful, "and it's like dog heaven at Jenny's cottage—he won't want to come home! Now, let's put our best outfits on quickly or we'll miss our train and be late for this wedding!"

CHAPTER FIVE

The van door opened with a clatter. "Come on, Alfie," Jenny said kindly. "Out you go. Come and meet the gang."

Alfie stayed on his beanbag, ears flopped forward and his paw over his nose, pretending that he wasn't really there. Jenny leaned in and pulled him out firmly.

Alfie looked around miserably. They were in the driveway of a small house with very high gates securely closed behind them, and an equally high fence enclosing the paved front yard. Jenny led Alfie into the house.

22

As soon as they opened the front door, a barrage of dogs appeared, hurling themselves at Jenny and sniffing the newcomer all over. Alfie cringed nervously in a corner.

"Okay, you guys," Jenny said, laughing. "Out you all go and make friends with our new boy."

She shooed them all through the living room and kitchen, which led directly into a paved backyard, also with a high fence around it. Alfie could see that escape was impossible. Meanwhile, the other inmates surged around him, barking and sniffing.

"How long are you in for?" asked a large, bouncing German shepherd named Boris.

"I don't know," said Alfie. "I don't even know why I'm here. I think it might be because I stole my boy's school sandwiches last week."

"*Oh* dear," barked a black-and-white border collie named Folly. "Sounds as if you might be in for life, then."

"*Life!*" gasped Alfie.

"Did you do anything else bad?" asked Folly.

"Only a *few* things," whimpered Alfie. "I suppose the worst was eating his mom's handbag."

"*Definitely* life, then!" said Folly, with a wink at Boris. "Don't you agree?"

"*Definitely*," woofed Boris. "They won't be wanting *you* back in a hurry."

"Oh, stop it, you two!" barked a dainty black-and-gray spaniel named Dixie. "You're frightening the life out of the poor darling. Don't listen to them, dear." She nuzzled up to Alfie and put a feathery paw on his huge knuckled foot. "We're only here for a little while: just a few days, or

a week, or sometimes longer, but they always come back for us. You'll see. We're only here while they're off doing people-things where we aren't allowed."

Jenny opened the door to the backyard and called everyone inside. She sat down on one of the two living room sofas, which were covered in rugs. After a few seconds, they were also covered in dogs, except for Alfie,

who was too nervous to barge his way in with the others. There were six dogs altogether: Alfie, Boris, Folly, Dixie, and two identical West Highland terriers who barked a lot— telling the bouncy Boris and the huge Alfie not to tread on them. One of the West Highland terriers settled, like a cat, onto

Jenny's lap. The other dogs did a lot of noisy leaping around, then collapsed into their regular places on the sofas. Jenny had brought Alfie's beanbag into the room and he curled up on it gratefully in a surprisingly tidy ball. He was so tired after all the frenzy that he began to drift off to sleep.

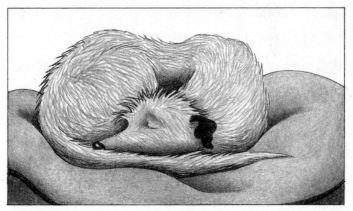

CHAPTER SIX

Aloud knocking set all the dogs barking and diving off the sofas to hurl themselves at the front door. They went crazy with delight when they saw it was Jenny's friend Rita, who always came with them for walks.

Alfie's ears sprang into the Full Rabbit as he woke with a start.

"Come in here, Rita," Jenny was saying. "We've got a baby deerhound staying with us. He's a bit nervous."

Alfie looked up mournfully from his beanbag.

"Oh, what a darling," said Rita, crouching down and smoothing his head. "Look at your funny ears! Don't worry, boy. We're

all heading off for a nice walk. Then there's dinner later and good friends to play with. It won't be five minutes before they come to take you back home again."

Jenny and Rita put all the dogs on their leashes. Jenny held on to the spaniel, the German shepherd, and Alfie, and Rita took the two West Highlands and the collie. When they left the front yard, Alfie saw that on one side they were next door to a farmhouse, surrounded by large fields, with lots of gray outbuildings and farm machinery parked in the concrete yard. On the other side was a normal road, full of cottages and parked cars, leading toward a railway station and a small parade of stores. It really was the very edge of the city.

The exercise field, which Charlie's mom had described, was next door to the farm. The dogs all knew where they were going and nearly yanked Jenny and Rita's arms out of their sockets as the field gate came into view. Alfie didn't pull; he hung back, trying to writhe his head out of his collar, but it was too tight to slip over his ears.

"We'll have to watch this one, Rita," called Jenny, bundling him through the gate with the others and bolting it behind them.

"Off you go!" she said, unclipping all their leashes.

"Run around!" said Rita briskly, as the three dogs she had been leading raced off to join Boris and Dixie.

"You too, Alfie!" called Jenny, pulling Alfie away from the gate by his collar. "Stretch those great long legs of yours."

They set off around the field, Alfie slinking along with them, inspecting the thick hedge for escape routes. He had noticed that there were areas farther up the field that looked as if the hedge might be thin enough to shoulder his way through.

Unfortunately, he hadn't noticed the wire, stretching between rough posts, set along the inside of the hedge all the way around the field. It was an electric wire, put there to keep cattle from breaking through the hedge in exactly the way that Alfie was planning to try. The wire was very rarely turned on, but on this particular day the farmer was planning to use the field for some of his cows and had turned it on only minutes before Jenny and Rita decided on their walk.

Alfie set off at a brisk run toward a gap that looked worth investigating. Dixie ran after him, barking joyfully.

"Glad you cheered up!" she called. "You can chase me if you want. I'll pretend to be a rabbit, then you can—"

"*Aark! Aark! Aark!* " Piercing yelps of pain burst from Alfie as his wet nose touched the wire. He couldn't believe it. The fence had bitten him. He zigzagged in a frenzy from right to left, barking and yelping. Jenny

and Rita were calling his name, trying to calm him down, but Alfie knew that he had to escape and the only way out was the way they had come in.

He ran headlong at the huge, barred gate, which loomed like a mountain as he approached it, gathering speed—thirty, thirty-five, and a final burst of forty miles per hour. Jenny and Rita clung to each other, watching in horror.

"He'll break his legs!" gasped Jenny. "He'll never get over it."

But he did.

Bunching his ultrastrong deerhound back legs at exactly the right moment, and tucking up his front legs as neatly as a gazelle, Alfie sailed above the topmost bar with inches to spare. He was out of sight within seconds, leaving Jenny and Rita speechless with shock.

CHAPTER SEVEN

Day turned to evening. Jenny and Rita had spent the whole day searching for Alfie.

First of all, they had taken the other dogs back to Jenny's house and Rita had called the police and the animal rescue centers, while Jenny began looking everywhere: around the farm buildings, in people's front yards, and in the children's playground nearby, finally arriving at the station end of the road. On either side of the station was a small parade of stores called Station Row, consisting of a corner shop selling all the usual things, an Italian restaurant called The Gondola, and a flower shop, with buckets containing bouquets of bright chrysanthemums and dark red roses, ready-wrapped for the train passengers to buy on their way home. The florist noticed Jenny peering into the station entrance and down the side alleys of the shops and came out to speak to her.

"You're not looking for a lost dog, are you?" she asked.

Jenny's heart exploded with joy. "Yes! Yes!" she exclaimed. "A huge gray dog—a deerhound."

"I saw it," the florist said firmly. "It *flew* past here about—oh, two hours ago. I've never *seen* such a big dog—and so *fast*—it was just a gray streak."

"Did you see where it went?" asked Jenny,

her heart plummeting when she realized how long ago he'd passed by.

"Yes, I did," said the florist. "It turned into the entrance to Hawkland Woods—just along there." She pointed it out helpfully, and Jenny thanked her and hurried to take a look. She peered through the parking area into the dense woodland beyond, then hurried back to collect Rita and the van, so they could start looking right away.

They were there for hours, calling Alfie's name until their voices gave out.

"Are you going to call the owners?" asked Rita.

"Not yet," said Jenny. "I'm *sure* we'll find him. He *must* be here somewhere."

"But it's getting dark," said Rita, "and Hawkland Woods is huge. There's *miles* of it. He could be right on the other side by now— you told me how fast a deerhound can run."

Jenny burst into tears. "We've just *got* to find him," she sobbed. "How can I ever face that young boy and tell him I've lost his dog?"

CHAPTER EIGHT

In the early evening gloom, a pair of foxes emerged from their den and sniffed the air to make sure there were no humans around. Their names were Fixit and Sunset.

"Don't you just love the autumn?" said Fixit as they trotted through the leafy carpet. "We're the same color as the leaves."

"So we are!" agreed Sunset. "Now we'll be able to hide even more easily."

"I think the weather's about to turn," said Fixit, pointing his nose upward and sniffing hard. "Look at those clouds."

Despite the perfect start to the day, a bank of ink-black clouds had suddenly appeared behind the treetops, moving fast in a sinister way, blown by a wind that had sprung up from nowhere. The branches were bending this way and that, sending showers of dry leaves turning and tumbling to the ground around them.

"What a shame," grumbled Sunset. "I was looking forward to a nice warm evening out hunting, and now we're going to get soaked."

"Not if we hurry," said Fixit. "It'll be dark

in five minutes. Let's go and check out the parade of stores that's near the edge of the woods. The people at The Gondola often forget to put the lid down on their garbage bins, and there might be enough leftovers for us to grab some quick takeout and get home before the rain sets in."

"Good idea, sweetheart," said Sunset fondly. "They don't call you Fixit for nothing. Race you there!"

There was one small van in the parking lot, and Jenny and Rita were just climbing into it when the two foxes arrived.

"Freeze!" said Fixit. He and Sunset stood motionless in the bushes as the two exhausted women got into the van.

Jenny sat down sideways in the driver's seat with the door open, blowing her nose. She stood up one last time and leaned on top of the van. "Alfie!" she yelled, her tearful voice whisked away by the rising wind.

"It's no use, Jen," called Rita. "It's nearly pitch-dark. We'll have to go home. Let's come out and try again at first light."

Fixit and Sunset watched as Jenny got back into the driver's seat and shut the door. The headlights suddenly sliced through the darkness as the van crunched over the gravel and away down the short track that led to the street.

Sunset looked at Fixit in the last remnants of grainy light. "I wonder who Alfie is?" she said.

"Well," said Fixit, "whoever he is, they're really upset about him."

CHAPTER NINE

A full-force storm had blown up over the city, a really bad one, with continual flashes of lightning, followed by deafening thunderclaps. Fixit and Sunset slunk through the undergrowth to their den, doing their best to keep out of the sideways-driving rain as they hurried back home.

"*Such* a good idea of yours, Fixit," said Sunset, licking her lips to catch the last morsel of Parmesan cheese from a pile of spaghetti Bolognese they had found in one of The Gondola's garbage bins.

Now, as they turned in through the dense thicket of bramble and bushes that led to their den, both foxes froze.

"Who's there?" growled Fixit in a low voice. "Come on out. I can smell you."

There was no reply in the rain-lashed, wind-howling darkness, but they both knew by the scent that another animal was there. They could also tell that it wasn't a fox or, indeed, a squirrel or badger, or any other animal you might expect to find in the wild nighttime woods.

"Show yourself," snarled Fixit, taking a cautious step toward the strange smell. As the two foxes peered into the darkness, they could just make out the shape of a huge, hairy creature, dripping water, its head bowed, shoulders hunched, shaking from head to foot. A surprisingly small whimper burst from the huge shape.

"Do you think it's a horse?" asked Sunset.

"Doesn't smell like a horse," said Fixit,

moving right up to the shape and sniffing hard. "Anyway, it's too small for a horse. It smells like a dog, but it's too big."

"Why don't you ask it what it is?" suggested Sunset, backing away so that Fixit was between herself and the enormous, quaking thing.

Fixit relaxed. He could tell by the trembling and whimpering, and by the smell emanating from the huge thing, that it was terrified and would not attack them.

"Come on now," he said, trying to sound firm but kind. "Pull yourself together and tell us what happened."

"What exactly *are* you?" asked Sunset, peeping around her husband.

The creature kept its face pointed at the floor but raised its ears, twisted them together, and flopped them over its forehead.

"I'm lost," it said.

"Yes, but what sort of *creature* are you?" continued Fixit.

"I'm a hound," mumbled Alfie—for it was Alfie who had run and run, escaping from the vicious fence until he felt far away enough to stop.

Sunset jumped back in alarm. "You're not a *fox*hound, are you?" she asked nervously.

"Of course he isn't, dear," said Fixit. "My cousin told me all about foxhounds. They're brown and white with floppy ears. You have very strange ears, don't you?" he continued, looking at Alfie's ears, which were now raised and folded neatly on top of his head like a pair of tea towels.

"Sorry," said Alfie, his teeth still chattering with fright. "I can't help it. My ears just do their own thing."

"Well," said Fixit briskly, preparing to enter the thicket. "Nice to meet you. Hope you find your way home."

There was a brilliant flash of lightning, lengthy enough for the two foxes to get a really good look at the sad, drenched bundle of misery hunched outside their front door. An earsplitting crack of thunder made them all jump out of their skins. Alfie shuffled close to Sunset and leaned on her so hard that she almost fell over.

"Steady now," said Fixit. "It's only thunder; it won't hurt you. Go on now—your people will be wondering where you are."

"No, they won't," sobbed Alfie. "They won't *know* where I am. My boy and his mom sent me away and left me with a lady I don't know. She took me to a field and the fence bit me. It was horrible! It bit me on the

nose and it went on and on hurting. I had to get away and then the lights went out and the sky exploded and now I don't know what to do. Please don't leave me on my own. *Please.*"

Fixit looked at Sunset and rolled his eyes. "We *would* invite you in," he said gently, "but you're too big to get inside—you'll just have to sleep here. Look, there's a dry area if you can get in deeper under this bush. We'll be nearby in our den and the storm will be over by morning. See that dark area just along there? That's our front entrance, so we won't be far away. We can work out how to get you home first thing in the morning."

"Thank you," whispered Alfie, still trying to cuddle up to Sunset, who was much smaller than he was.

"Come along, then, dear," said Fixit to Sunset. "We're all soaked through."

"I can't move," said Sunset. "The great big lump is sitting on my tail."

"Sorry," said Alfie, not moving. He closed his eyes tightly, hoping it was all a bad dream.

"Now look here, friend," said Fixit sternly. "You're going to have to pull yourself together. Up you go. That's it, back in under the nice dry bush—that's right—and we'll sort it all out in the morning."

Alfie crouched as low as he could and backed into the space the foxes had shown him.

"You *will* come back in the morning?" he whimpered. "You won't just leave me here?"

"Oh, for goodness' *sake*!" exclaimed Fixit. "Our home is right next to you—you can see the entrance from here. You ought to be ashamed of yourself, a great big hound like you behaving like a puppy."

"But I *am* a puppy," explained Alfie. "I'm just big. It's not my fault I'm big. I wish I weren't. I wish I were home with my boy. He lets me sleep on his bed sometimes. I'll be *so* nice to our cat if I ever get home again."

He began to yelp and howl at the same time, making a noise like a sea lion at feeding time.

"Stop it! Stop it at once!" ordered Fixit. "Or you'll have to move on from here. It's not the storm you have to worry about, my boy, it's humans. There are hunters out in this forest at night, out to shoot us foxes."

"Sorry," said Alfie, taking a deep breath

and forcing himself to calm down. "You *will* come and get me in the morning?"

"Don't start *that* again," said Fixit, ushering Sunset toward the den entrance. "I told you already. We'll be back at first light—now stop your noise and go to sleep. Good *night*."

"See you in the morning," Sunset called over her shoulder as she entered the tunnel, followed by Fixit, leaving Alfie alone in the creaking, moaning, wind-torn woods.

CHAPTER TEN

"I have something to tell you, Charlie," said Charlie's mom as they opened the front door to their house, home from their night away.

Charlie suddenly realized that his mom was looking very anxious.

"What is it, Mom?" he asked. "Did something happen?"

They were still standing inside the front door. His mom had picked up the letters from the mat and was holding them tightly, looking at the floor.

"Yes, it did," she said, looking up at him and trying to look like a person in control. "I'm afraid Alfie got lost yesterday morning."

Charlie's mouth fell open in horror. "Yesterday morning!" he exclaimed. "But that means he was out all night in the storm. He's petrified of storms. He's petrified of *everything*! He doesn't even like the door banging shut—and he hates getting wet— he won't go for a *walk* if it's raining. Oh, Mom! Where is he? How are we going to find him?"

Charlie's mom put an arm around him and led him into the kitchen so that she could put the kettle on and make a reassuring cup of tea.

"Now don't go getting worked up," she said soothingly. "I called Jenny on the train home while you were snoozing and she told me what happened. Unfortunately, that nice safe field I saw had an electric wire fence around the hedge because they sometimes keep cattle in there. Alfie got a shock from it and managed to leap over the gate. Jenny and her friend spent the whole day looking for him and they're out again now, at this very moment, trying to find him. I'm *sure* they will. He's so big now, someone's bound to notice him.

"Meanwhile, we can print some posters and go around pinning them up near the stores. He'll be very easy to identify, especially with his ears half done."

The cat-flap banged and Florence barged

through, meowing and twining herself around Charlie's ankles. Charlie picked her up and held her tight. "At least we still have you," he said. "Don't *you* go running off anywhere."

"Of *course* not," purred Florence, snuggling down in Charlie's arms. "Why on earth would I want to do that?"

CHAPTER ELEVEN

Hawkland Woods was covered in a thick carpet of wet leaves after the terrible night before. Whole branches were strewn around, some of the streams had risen and overflowed into small lakes, and in between everything was a layer of squelching mud.

Fixit and Sunset crouched on either side of Alfie under the bush where they had left him the night before. True to their word, they had come out at the very first paling of the sky to see if they could get rid of the enormous and rather embarrassing creature they had somehow gotten stuck with. They had peered under the bush hoping he might be gone, but he was very much still there, hunched in the same shivering huddle, both ears curving sideways toward them, resembling a pair of wind-blown trees. (See Earstyle 3.)

"Well, then," said Fixit in a rather forced jolly tone. "Here we all are again."

"Wind's dying down," said Sunset, "and the rain's stopped. I expect you'll be feeling a bit hungry."

"Not really," said Alfie.

"What sort of hound *are* you?" asked Fixit, lying flat in front of the bush so that he could see properly into Alfie's face.

"Perhaps he's a type of anteater," said Sunset. "You know, a sort of *ant*hound. He's got a very long nose. Show us your tongue."

Alfie opened his mouth and rolled out his tongue like it was a strip of bacon.

"Perhaps not," said Fixit. "What's your name? You must have a name. Mine's Fixit, by the way, and this is my wife, Sunset."

"My name is Alfie," said Alfie glumly.

"Alfie!" exclaimed Sunset. "That was

the name those people were calling in the parking lot last night."

"Do you think they might still be there?" asked Alfie hopefully.

"Sorry, friend," said Fixit, "they were just leaving when we saw them, but they *did* seem very upset that they'd lost you. Are you sure you're a hound?"

"I *think* so,' said Alfie. "I *think* I might be a sort of *loved* hound."

"A *love* hound!" Both foxes laughed together.

"No," said Alfie, "a *loved* hound. My boy used to call me his darling dear deerhound, so I suppose I'm a very much *loved* hound."

"Well, I've never heard of a 'loved hound' before," said Fixit. "Anyway, hounds are always good at chasing things, whatever type they are."

"As long as you don't chase *us*," warned Sunset.

"Of *course* I won't," said Alfie. "I've taken

a vow that I'll never chase any animal ever again. Our cat, Florence, made me do it. I promised."

"I don't know how you're going to eat, then," mused Fixit. "You'll have to go hunting if you don't want to starve."

"I'll be all right," explained Alfie. "My dinner always comes in a can."

Sunset and Fixit exchanged hopeless glances.

"There aren't many cans in the middle of Hawkland Woods," said Sunset.

"No can openers either," agreed Fixit. "Come on, friend. Come on out and stretch your legs."

Alfie crawled from under his bush and stood up. Both foxes gazed up in amazement. He was at least twice as tall as they were.

All three animals had a good sniff of one another. "You smell really nice," Alfie said shyly. "Sort of pungent and putrid."

"Thanks," said Sunset. "*We* like it."

"You can roll in this messy patch outside our door," offered Fixit. "Then we'll all smell the same."

"Gosh, thanks!" said Alfie, throwing himself, shoulder first, onto the ground.

Sunset and Fixit smiled at each other as they watched their strange guest rolling from side to side, waving his endless legs in the air.

They gave him a thorough sniffing when he finally stood up again.

"Great!" said Sunset. "Now you smell just like a fox."

"Excellent!" agreed Fixit. "Let's go and see what we can find for breakfast. The café's a good place to try after a storm. The trash cans will be all over the place—saves us the trouble of knocking them over."

CHAPTER TWELVE

The scene at the café was better than they could have hoped for. All three of the trash cans had been blown onto their sides, spilling out drenched sandwich crusts, half-eaten burgers, and waterlogged fries. Alfie was thrilled to find a whole ham and cheese sandwich and half of a cheese Danish.

"This is great!" he woofed happily, his spirits lifting for the first time since the horror of the fence.

"There's a whole load of sausages in this one!" Sunset called gleefully, half-hidden inside the can.

Suddenly there was a series of short sharp yaps from Fixit. "Quick! Out! Someone's coming!" he warned.

They were through the open gate and into the undergrowth just as car headlights swept like prison searchlights across the strewn garbage and upturned tables. The morning was so gloomy that the car needed lights to make its way across the tree-lined road. The car stopped and the café's owners, Ken and Rosemary, climbed out.

"What a mess," said Ken. "We'd better get started before any customers arrive."

"I don't think there'll be many customers today!" Rosemary laughed. "You'd have to be crazy to go for a walk in the woods after a night like that—oh, look, there *are* people coming up the trail! I'd better go and open up in case they need a cup of coffee."

The customers were Charlie and his mom, who had teamed up with Rita and Jenny. True to their word, Jenny and Rita had been up with the watery sun, calling Alfie's name against the dawn chorus and dying wind in the creaking, clattering branches. Charlie and his mom had arrived to join them, armed with bundles of posters showing Alfie, brushed and smart, sitting on a sofa and looking rather elegant.

Charlie was wearing his sneakers with lights in the heels to brighten the gloomy morning, and also, as he explained to Rita and Jenny, so that Alfie could see them if he was in the bushes somewhere.

They had worked steadily for an hour, tacking posters to trees and calling Alfie's name, before deciding to check out the little café in the very center of the square.

"I hope it's open," said Charlie's mom. "It's only nine thirty and they might not be open at all after such a dreadful storm."

"Yes, they are, Mom!" said Charlie. "I can see them through the trees—look!"

Ken and Rosemary were only too happy to put up a poster and promised to keep an eye out for the missing deerhound. They were so kind and friendly that the band of Alfie-hunters decided to stop for breakfast. Charlie's mom could tell how miserable he was because he couldn't eat anything at all, not even something from the plate of muffins and cookies she had ordered to try to take his mind off things.

"No thanks," he said politely as Jenny tried to tempt him with a chocolate-chip cookie. "Do you think we're ever going to find him?"

Jenny's eyes filled with tears. "I'm *so* sorry," she said with heartfelt remorse. "I never thought *any* dog could jump a gate as high as that."

Charlie's mom patted Jenny's shoulder. "Come on," she said. "It's no one's fault. Let's keep looking before it starts raining again. He's got to be here somewhere."

CHAPTER THIRTEEN

At that precise moment, Alfie was half a mile away, back under his bush, wishing that he hadn't dropped the cheese Danish when they had made their quick exit from the café.

Fixit and Sunset had gone into their den for a morning snooze.

"What on earth are we going to do with him, dear?" asked Sunset, resting her head on Fixit's neck. "He'll starve if he won't hunt."

"Don't ask *me*," replied Fixit. "He's a liability, what with all the noise he makes and the size of him. I suppose we could take him to The Gondola later on, or perhaps we could share our dinner with him if we have a good night's hunting."

"You're so generous," said Sunset admiringly.

"Not really," said Fixit, "but we're sort of stuck with him at the moment and we can't let the poor thing go hungry."

Under his bush, Alfie had fallen asleep. The morning passed by and in his dreams he heard Charlie calling his name. "*Alfie! Alfie!* Here, boy! Here!"

It was so real that he woke with a start, ears doing the Full Rabbit. He changed ear position to Wind-Blown Tree, first to the left, then to the right, but there was

no sound except the rustling leaves, which descended in drifts from the trees above him. "It must have been a dream," he thought sadly, and drifted back to sleep.

Only a few bushes away, Charlie had been calling as loudly as he could. "*Alfie! Alfie!* Here, boy! Here!" over and over.

"That's enough, darling," said his mom. "You'll lose your voice in a minute. We'll put

up some more posters in the stores by the station and in that nice Italian restaurant, and then we should head home for a while and get some rest. We can come back tomorrow and search over the other side of the wooded area while you're at school."

"Oh, Mo-om!" said Charlie. "I *can't* go to school when Alfie's still lost!"

"Sorry, love," said Charlie's mom. "You can't miss school *whatever* the reason. Anyway, we'll have to get home now or you'll never get up in the morning."

"I'll keep looking until it gets dark," said Jenny.

"Me too," said Rita.

"Okay, then," said Charlie's mom. "Let's meet up tomorrow—call me if you find him!"

"Of course," said Jenny, trying to sound optimistic, though her heart was down in her muddy rain boots.

CHAPTER FOURTEEN

"**W**hat *are* we going to do with him?" asked Sunset, snuggled up next to Fixit in the earthy darkness of their den.

"Well, he can't stay outside *our* door much longer," said Fixit grumpily, "*that's* for sure."

"Perhaps we could dig an extra-large den next to ours and sort of adopt him," suggested Sunset. "He's so *helpless*."

"I don't think so, dear," said Fixit fondly. "A sweet thought, but not very practical. Right now I'm a bit hungry—let's go and see if it's dark yet."

Outside, Alfie had come out of his bush and was lying right next to their entrance. He was well camouflaged in the early evening gloom, lying very still among the tangled gray brambles and piles of dusty-looking leaves.

"I haven't moved for ages," he said proudly. "I'm practicing being just like a fox."

"*Just* like a fox," agreed Sunset, licking his nose affectionately. "Well done, dear."

"Smells like a fox too," said Fixit, giving Alfie's filthy coat an appreciative sniff.

"What's for dinner?" asked Alfie. "I'm starving."

They decided to head for the garbage bins at the back of The Gondola for an easy meal. Fixit and Sunset knew that the garbage collection was the next morning, so the bins would be perfect for rummaging through. On the way, they taught Alfie how to slink along, keeping to the side of any open spaces, stopping to check all around, then freezing if anything rustled, always

taking a few quick steps at a time. Alfie's radarlike ears were very helpful in the lookout process. He proudly showed his new friends Listen Both Ways, where he could listen in front and behind at the same

time, and how he could hide behind a bush and bend his nose around a corner to sniff for anyone coming, like a nasal periscope.

"You must admit he's got some really useful tricks, Mr. F," said Sunset, impressed.

"True, my dear," said Fixit. "Pity he's so huge, or he'd make a very good honorary fox."

They reached a place where the woodland stopped abruptly and an area of short grass led to the back of the parade of stores. There were a few clumps of bushes and a pond with some benches around it. A tarmac path led from an alley between the restaurant and the flower shop across the grass to some houses on the other side, and you could see the bridge across the railway track leading to the far station platform. Streetlights along the edge of the path cast an orange glow over everything.

A train suddenly clattered into the station just as the little group was skittering a few paces from a ragged elderflower bush to a low mass of brambles.

"Don't move!" ordered Fixit. "Drop down, Alfie, and freeze. People often walk across this path after a train. Don't move till I say."

They all kept completely still, Alfie flat on the grass with his ears over his eyes, trying not to panic as the noisy train rattled and hissed out of the station.

"Okay, team," said Fixit, "they're all gone. Good timing, actually. There won't be another train for half an hour, and the kitchen porter's just been out and put a load of stuff in the bin, so *he* won't be out for another hour. Come on—let's go for it."

CHAPTER FIFTEEN

The two huge garbage bins at the back of The Gondola were even more bountiful than the ones at the café. To Alfie's utter joy, all the leftovers were dredged with cheese— cheese pasta, cheese pizzas, even the meat leftovers were dusted with a dreamy coating of grated Parmesan. It was deerhound heaven. Alfie stood on his hind legs, knocked open the hinged lid, and dragged out delicious pieces of garlic chicken and clumps of spaghetti, dropping them onto ground level for Fixit and Sunset.

"He really *is* a help with these huge bins," said Fixit, gulping down as much as possible.

Within a few minutes, the top layer was dragged out and scattered on the ground or eaten. Alfie craned his neck to look in and saw nearly an entire pepperoni pizza wedged farther down. He scrabbled his front paws

noisily over the side of the bin and stretched his neck until it almost dislocated, trying to reach the prized pizza.

"Steady, Alf," warned Sunset. "Too much noise!"

Too late. Alfie lost his balance and plunged headfirst into the bin, which fell over sideways with a deafening clatter.

"Run!" barked Fixit.

The two foxes shot across the clearing and into the woodland as Alfie, panicking, yelped and scrambled, trying to turn around inside the bin, before backing out, spaghetti

and pizza topping dangling from his head like a hat. He raced as fast as his trembling legs would carry him into the woods and followed the scent of Sunset and Fixit back to their den, where he received a stern talking-to from his guardians.

At the back of The Gondola, Marco, the young busboy, had come out to investigate, peering into the gloomy woods beyond the clearing.

"What was the noise?" asked Lorenzo, one of the waiters, who had also come out to see what the commotion was.

"It was a dog," said Marco. "I caught a glimpse of it as it ran into the woods—a huge, gray dog, just like the one on the poster."

CHAPTER SIXTEEN

When something awful has happened, one of the worst moments is waking from a deep, exhausted sleep, having forgotten—just for a brief instant—whatever it was that has ruined everything.

When morning and the awful moment came, Charlie crawled out of bed and came downstairs, sniffing and rubbing his eyes, trying really hard not to cry. His mom took one look at him and changed her mind about sending him to school.

After breakfast, Charlie's mom found him in the front yard, hanging over the gate, staring down the road.

"What are you doing?" she asked.

"I'm sending out thought waves," said Charlie, still staring into the distance, not turning to look at his mom. "They're magic thought waves—like radio waves—so he'll know we're still looking. We'll find him, Mom. I don't know how, but we *will* find him. I know it!"

Charlie's mom felt her eyes fill with tears. "Oh, darling," she said, standing close behind him and wrapping him in her arms. "You know, there is a tiny chance that we won't be able to find him."

"Don't say that, Mom," said Charlie, trying to stop his voice from trembling. "You can't even *think* it, or the thought waves won't work."

At that very moment, the telephone began to ring and they rushed inside to answer it.

"This is Lorenzo Bertolli," said a voice with an Italian accent. "I'm calling about the lost dog. Is this the right number?"

"Yes!" said Charlie's mom.

"We think we saw your dog last night," said Lorenzo. "Around the back of our restaurant, The Gondola—you know, by the station. You came and put up a poster yesterday."

"How fantastic!" said Charlie's mom, her heart dancing with hope. "Did you catch him?"

"I'm afraid not," said Lorenzo, "but he'd had a very good meal from our garbage bins, so at least he's not going hungry! He'll probably be back again tonight. Perhaps you'd like to come and keep watch."

"You bet we will!" said Charlie's mom. "Thank you *so* much for calling."

"You *see*, Mom!" said Charlie, dancing around the kitchen. "The thought waves are working already."

"They certainly *seem* to be!" said Charlie's mom. "We can spend the afternoon putting up more posters, then we can have spaghetti Bolognese at the restaurant and spend the rest of the evening lurking by the garbage bins!"

That first evening at the restaurant was so very full of hope. Everyone had spent the day doing positive things. Jenny and Rita had put up posters and called for Alfie all around one side of the forest, while Charlie and his mom did the other side and checked the little café to see if anyone had noticed anything, which they hadn't. Then they all met at The Gondola in the early evening for a well-deserved meal. It was the first time that Charlie had felt hungry since Alfie had been lost.

"I just *know* he's going to turn up tonight!" he announced happily, scarfing down loops of spaghetti Bolognese. "He's so clever he even knew where to get some cheese! Trust a deerhound to find the best restaurant in town for his dinner!"

CHAPTER SEVENTEEN

ack at the foxes' den, the strange trio was getting ready for their night's hunting.

"Can't we just go back to that nice place with the cheesy garbage?" asked Alfie. "There's sure to be some good stuff there."

"Not tonight," said Fixit. "The garbage men always collect on a Monday. Any leftovers would be right at the bottom of the bin, and we can't risk you falling in after yesterday's disaster. Anyway, they'll be on the lookout tonight, so we'll have to skip it for a few days."

"But I'm not allowed to—you know—
chase anything," explained Alfie desperately.
"I promised on my honor and I might forget
when I go home again. Suppose I get *so* used
to hunting that I chase Florence! Suppose
I *eat Florence*! Charlie would be *so* upset—so
would Florence!"

"No one's expecting you to eat a *cat* for
goodness' sake," said Sunset, exasperated.
"Only a rabbit—there're loads of rabbits."

"I can't hunt rabbits either," said Alfie,
shocked. "The girl next door's got a rabbit
named Blanche. I might get so used to
hunting rabbits that I jump over the fence
and *eat Blanche* and then everyone will be
mad!"

"Well, you'll be lucky to find any leftovers tonight," said Fixit. "There's nothing on Garbage Day, so it's hunt or go hungry."

"I'll just stay here under my bush, then, if you don't mind," said Alfie.

"Suit yourself," said Sunset. "See you later."

At the back of The Gondola, hidden behind the boxes and crates, Rita, Jenny, Charlie, and his mom sat perfectly still, eyes trained on the bushes and woods, willing Alfie to appear like a gray ghost and make his way across the soft, orange-lit grass. Trains rattled in and out of the station, people walked down the pathway between the stores and the houses, a hedgehog came out from beneath a bush and snuffled around in the half light, but there was no other sign of animal life. Marco brought out the final bag of garbage to put in the bin. The last train rattled into the station and the platform lights went out.

Disappointment settled on the shoulders of the band of searchers like a damp overcoat as they wished each other good night.

"I really, *really* thought he'd come," said Charlie, bursting into tears as he and his mom climbed wearily into their car. "Oh, Mom. Where on *earth* can he be?"

CHAPTER EIGHTEEN

Days turned into weeks. In the early days, several people called to say that they had seen a dog like the one on the poster. One of them was an old lady who had a big house with a yard that looked out onto the woods. She said that she had seen a huge, gray dog sneaking out of her yard very early one morning carrying half a loaf of bread that she'd put out for the birds. Charlie and his mom rushed over to the old lady's house and spent hours calling, but there was no sign of him.

Three other people called with sightings of the poster dog, but all of them said that he had run off into the bushes and no one got anywhere near catching him.

Jenny and Rita visited the animal rescue homes every week, with dwindling hope. The posters began to fade.

One morning, two men were out walking their old mutt and stopped to look at a ragged poster flapping on a tree. "Wow!" said Stan. "Look at that, Bert. Do you think it's still out here somewhere? A young deerhound, king of the hounds—just think what we could do with one of those when we go out hunting, especially as old Lightning here's a bit past his prime."

Lightning raised one ear and dropped it again.

"Sorry, old boy," continued Stan, scratching the top of Lightning's head affectionately. "You were the best in your day."

They stopped and read the poster all the way through. "It's been up for several weeks," said Bert. "His name's Alfie. They probably found him ages ago."

"Wouldn't hurt to keep an eye out, though, would it?" said Stan. "Just in case."

Charlie wouldn't give up. He still hung over the front gate every day before he went to school, sending out his magic thought waves. His mom could hardly bear to watch him. It was difficult to keep believing that such a nervous, comfort-loving dog could survive for so long out in the wild winter woods all by himself—but, of course, he *wasn't* all by himself.

Back at the foxes' den, Alfie and the foxes had settled into a routine. Despite all their attempts to persuade him, Alfie refused point-blank to hunt. So while his friends were out pursuing rabbits, he sneaked off to raid the café trash cans at first light and rummage at The Gondola in the early hours, when the restaurant was closed and everyone was in bed. Sometimes the foxes went with him, but he was less terrified now and often went alone, easily tracing the route from their den, creeping along with much careful stopping and starting, just as they had taught him. Sadly, he often went on a night when Charlie and his mom had been there, sometimes with Jenny and Rita, keeping one of their vigils, but neither Alfie nor his band of faithful searchers realized that they had missed each other by hours.

"My collar's getting really tight," said Alfie one evening as they all lay outside the den, waiting for complete darkness so they could set off on their various food-collecting missions.

"Let's take a look," said Sunset.

Alfie sat up and stretched his neck.

"You're right, my boy," said Fixit, peering up at the young dog. He was growing really tall, and although he was thin, the collar had become so tight that it was cutting into his neck. "We'd better get this off, or it'll strangle you. Lie down, so I can reach it—goodness, you're getting so huge!"

Fixit levered his lower jaw under the collar, clamped his upper jaw on top, and began chewing at the leather. It was hard work and after a while he gave up and Sunset took over. They both worked patiently, taking

turns as they tried to bite through the tough leather. Finally, on Fixit's fourth attempt, the collar fell off. Alfie shook his head from side to side.

"Thank you so much," he said politely. "That feels much better."

"What shall we do with it?" asked Sunset, prodding the broken collar with her paw.

"I'll take it into my bush, if you don't mind," said Alfie, "as a sort of souvenir of who I was—just in case I forget."

CHAPTER NINETEEN

Weeks turned into months. All the leaves came off the trees in the late autumn gales. Alfie hated the storms and cowered under his bush, trying to remember the beanbag in the kitchen with Florence snuggled up next to him, and, best of all, Charlie sneaking him onto his own bed for the night and stroking his ears and singing to him.

It all seemed so long ago and far away, and now the café was closing for the winter. The only place with food would be The Gondola's garbage bins, which were sometimes closed too tightly to get them open without making a lot of noise, so Alfie often went hungry.

One morning Fixit and Sunset came and prodded Alfie awake, which was unusual as the foxes usually slept during the day, especially in the early morning.

"What's up?" asked Alfie.

"Well," said Sunset excitedly, "we went past the café early this morning and guess what—there's a poster of you stuck up on the bulletin board by the tables. It was half hidden behind a tree, but now that all the leaves are off you can see it clearly."

"Are you sure it's me?" asked Alfie.

"Very sure," said Fixit. "It's got a big picture of you wearing your red collar, sitting on a sofa. The sofa's green and it's got big orange flowers on it."

"That's it!" barked Alfie. "That's definitely our sofa! It *must* be me!"

"You look much *cleaner* in the poster than you do now," said Sunset, "but it's definitely you. Why don't you go and sit next to your picture when there are some people there? The café always shuts for the winter, so this weekend might be your last chance."

"What a good idea," said Fixit.

They chose a Saturday afternoon. By a twist of fate, Charlie and his mom had gone there for lunch to say good-bye to Rosemary and

Ken before they closed for the season. Charlie was very glum. He could tell that the grown-ups were losing interest, and although his mom still came out with him and checked the usual places from time to time, she was beginning to say things like, "We can't keep this up forever" and "Perhaps some nice kind person's taken him home." She didn't even want to have dinner at The Gondola, even though the friendly waiters always gave them a discount because they came there so often.

Only twenty minutes after Charlie and his mom had left the café, the two foxes and Alfie slunk silently into the bushes that came right up to the fence surrounding the tables and chairs. A family of two little girls,

LOST

a baby in a stroller, and their mom and dad were just settling themselves at a table, which was conveniently right next to the poster of Alfie. They were all warmly dressed and had decided to sit outside. The dad went inside to order their food, but then one of the girls asked for something else, so the mom hurried inside, keeping an eye on the children through the big plate-glass window while she relayed the change of order to her husband.

"Now!" said Fixit. "Just go and sit next to the poster and someone will come and rescue you."

"Do you *really* think so?" asked Alfie.

"Absolutely," said Sunset. "Go on, dear. I'm so glad you'll get home to your people at last."

Alfie hesitated. "I'll miss you," he mumbled.

"Just *go*," said Fixit. "It's for the best."

So Alfie went. The little gate was closed, but he leaped over it easily, sidled up to the poster, and sat down next to it, looking hopefully at the children.

CHAPTER TWENTY

For various reasons, everything went completely wrong. For starters, after all this time, Alfie didn't look anything like the tidy, brushed young dog with a smart red collar that was on the poster. His facial fur was slick and greasy from all the garbage-rooting and his body fur had grown much longer and was intertwined with bits of brambles and leaves. He was encrusted with slabs of dried mud from where he lay each night in his muddy nest under the bush, and his ears, described on the poster as "one black and one gray and furry," had both grown scruffy and looked exactly the same. Worst of all, he had no collar.

Adding to the horror of his unkempt appearance, Alfie unfortunately decided to smile. The trouble with a deerhound smile is that it looks exactly the same as a deerhound snarl. The two little girls sat mesmerized with terror, as what seemed to be the big bad wolf from a fairy tale sprang over the fence, sat down right next to their table, and bared its teeth at them. Just as they began to scream, their parents came rushing to their aid, hurling sandwiches and shouting furiously.

"Get away!" yelled the dad. "Don't you touch my girls!"

Alfie waved a paw, trying to look charming, before he realized that everyone was yelling at him, so he ran for it and leaped back over the gate. The dad threw another sandwich,

which Alfie, with astonishing presence of mind, caught in midair and carried off into the undergrowth, where he vanished in seconds.

Rosemary came rushing out of the café. "Hang on a moment," she said to the

distraught parents, who were cuddling their weeping daughters—even the baby had woken up and was screaming its head off—"I think it was the dog from this poster. Perhaps it was scrounging for food."

"Well, it looked vicious to *me*," said the mom angrily.

"So sorry," said Rosemary. "I'll get you some more sandwiches to replace the ones he stole."

She ran inside and told Ken, "It was definitely him. I just can't believe it after all this time, but it *was* a huge, gray dog—a bit rough-looking, but then he's been wild for two-and-a-half months, so he won't be looking like an entrant for Westminster."

"I expect the boy and his mom are nearby," said Ken. "I'll call them on their cell phone and tell them what happened."

As soon as they heard the news, Charlie and his mom raced back to the café. They hunted around the whole area, calling and calling. It started to rain, lightly at first, followed by a spectacular cloudburst. Charlie didn't even notice. He continued pushing his way into the bushes as far as he could, shouting for his dog. "Alfie, *Alfie!*" he yelled. "Come on! Pretty please! *Pleeease* come out, Alfie! It's me! ALFIE!"

Ken and Rosemary insisted that they sit down for a snack and rest. Charlie and his mom looked as if someone had been pouring buckets of water over them.

"It's just not *fair*!" said Charlie. "If we'd only come for our lunch later, we would've got him. Now he'll be scared after everyone shouted at him."

"The little girls were scared because he snarled at them," explained Ken.

"He wasn't *snarling*!" said Charlie. "He was

smiling at them. He's always smiling. He was right next to his poster—he was trying to tell them who he was."

"Are we *sure* it was him?" asked Charlie's mom.

"He really did fit the bill," said Rosemary. "A huge, gray, scruffy dog—didn't have a collar, though."

"Maybe it was hidden under his fur," insisted Charlie. "I *know* it was him. We can't just *leave* him, Mom."

"Okay," said his mom. "Let's go home and change, then come back to The Gondola for our dinner and stake out the garbage bins at the back. Lorenzo said there's definitely been garbage-raiding activity going on. If it really was him here today, he might try The Gondola later on tonight."

CHAPTER TWENTY-ONE

Back at the den, Alfie had curled up under his bush, which was dripping unpleasantly with rainwater. He was shaking with cold and Sunset had wedged herself in, trying to comfort him.

"I think it was the smile that did it," she said. "People are so stupid. They don't know the difference between a smile and a snarl. Your boy would know."

"But he doesn't know where I am," whimpered Alfie. "They're *never* going to find me. I'm lost forever—the Hound of Hawkland Woods. I might as well start learning to hunt. No one cares what I do; no one's ever going to pet me again."

He began to yelp, then stopped because he was now foxy enough to know he should keep quiet. "Where's Fixit?"

"He went back to pick up the first bunch of sandwiches they threw," said Sunset. "They went over your head and into the bushes—a lot of them—too good to waste."

The undergrowth rustled and Fixit appeared beside them with the sandwiches. He had been running fast and sat down panting. "Good news, Alf!" he said. "*Really* good news."

Alfie curved his ears in Fixit's direction. "I'm listening," he said.

When Fixit had sneaked back to retrieve the sandwiches from a dense tangle of brambles, Charlie and his mom had emerged from the café and stopped to say good-bye to Ken and Rosemary. Fixit had stayed utterly still and waited, and while he waited, he overheard their conversation.

"It *must* have been your Alfie at The Gondola," Ken was saying. "There can't be two deerhounds lost in the woods. Good luck tonight. I really hope you manage to catch him."

"It's worth a try," said Charlie's mom.

"What time are you going?" asked Rosemary. "Ken and I might join you. We close here at four. We could celebrate our last weekend of the season."

"That would be great," said Charlie's mom. "We'll go at seven. See you there."

Fixit excitedly relayed all this to Alfie. "They were definitely your people!" he barked. "A lady with straight brown hair and a young boy. They'll be at The Gondola tonight at seven! All you have to do is go and stand outside the window. *They* won't go crazy if you smile at them—they *know* you. They're looking for you."

"I can't tell the time," said Alfie. "How will I know when they're there?"

"Do they have a car?" asked Sunset.

"Yes!" said Alfie. "A red one with a lift-up door at the back. They can put the backseats down to fit me in."

"Well, there you are, then," said Fixit. "You'll see it parked outside, and you'll know they're in there. Anyway, I'm really good at judging what time it is—I have a sort of feel for it, so we can set off when I *feel* it's the right time and you can check the cars to make sure—okay?"

Gradually, Alfie began to perk up. He allowed himself to imagine pressing his furry face against the window. He imagined Charlie seeing him and shouting for joy and rushing outside and crushing him in his arms, and Charlie's mom jumping up and down, and Alfie doing his sea-lion yelps of delight. It would be such a relief to be home again—dinners out of a can, the warm, squishy beanbag—he wouldn't even mind a good bath and a brushing session. Thank goodness he'd kept his promise to Florence.

They shared the sandwiches as soon as night fell. The two foxes always shared as much as they could, especially as they could see that Alfie was very thin.

"It's time," said Fixit, a while after nightfall. "They'll be there by now. It's around seven. I can feel it in my bones. You'll be safe to go and check for their car."

"We'll come with you to the edge of the woods," said Sunset.

At the edge of the woodland, with the pond clearing spread out in front of them, Fixit and Sunset said good-bye to their unlikely lodger.

"Thank you for taking care of me," said Alfie. "Thank you for being my friends."

"Don't mention it," said Fixit kindly. "You've turned into a really great honorary fox. Been a pleasure having you on our team."

Sunset stepped forward and leaned her head on Alfie's side. He bent his long neck and rested his head on top of hers.

"Good-bye, then," said Alfie, stepping onto the grass.

He turned to tell them to stay safe, but they had already vanished into the rustling undergrowth.

CHAPTER TWENTY-TWO

Alfie looked around cautiously so that he could check all the usual things. There was no train arriving, no busboy coming out, no owner taking a dog for a walk. In fact, there was no one at all; everything was quiet. He set off cautiously toward the alley at the side of The Gondola; only a few paces and he'd see them on the other side of the glass, their faces full of utter happiness when they saw him, their own dog, safe at last.

Alfie stopped at the mouth of the alleyway. At the other end he could see part of a parked car. It was red and looked just like his people's car. Alfie's heart lurched with relief—they were there! He could also see that the streetlights were much stronger at the far end of the alley. All his fox-learned caution came into play. He raised his front paw, almost in slow motion, lowered his head, and raised his ears in Extreme Listening Mode. There was no sound at all; it seemed safe.

Alfie set off down the alley, heart pounding, one step—then stop; two skittering steps—then stop. Halfway down, feeling

hemmed in by the two buildings that made up the side walls of the alleyway, Alfie stopped altogether to listen.

Suddenly, a man turned into the alleyway from the street entrance. With truly dreadful timing it was Stan, who was returning from the corner shop with a can of dog food for Lightning's dinner.

Stan stopped, his arms by his sides, not moving at all. Alfie didn't move either. They both stood looking at each other, like a standoff scene in a cowboy movie.

Very slowly, Stan put his hand into his pocket and brought out the can of dog food. *Very* slowly, he pulled the ring on top of the can and peeled back the lid.

A marvelous waft of beef sailed through the air into Alfie's famished nostrils. Beef! His all-time favorite, even more wonderful than cheese.

"Hey there, Alfie," called Stan, in a low, gentle voice. "Hey, Alfie. Here's some dinner for you. Here, Alfie."

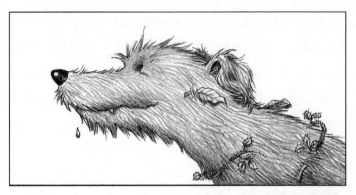

"He knows who I am!" thought Alfie. "He knows my name and he's brought my favorite food! Maybe my boy sent him to get me!"

Taking great care to move very slowly, Stan bent down and scooped the beef out of the can with his fingers into a heap on the pavement. Then he moved two paces back. "There you are, Alfie," said Stan in his soft, friendly voice. "All for you."

It was too much for the poor ravenous creature—smelling the wonderful smell, hearing his own name spoken so kindly. He forgot everything the foxes had taught him, ran up the alley, and dived onto the food.

Immediately, Stan sprang into action. He had a rope leash in his pocket, which he whipped out and dropped over Alfie's head. Alfie didn't even notice at first because he was so busy frantically wolfing down every last morsel of the heavenly dog food, but as soon as Stan pulled the rope tight, total panic set in. Alfie tried everything, twirling around, standing on his hind legs, trying

to jerk the leash out of his captor's hands, but Stan knew how to handle dogs. He walked forcefully down the alley, back into the pond clearing, yanking Alfie so hard that he had no choice but to follow; it was either that or be strangled by the tightening leash. At the same time, he continued talking to Alfie in such a persuasive but firm voice that Alfie couldn't help wondering if the man really *did* know him from his old life and had come to help him.

"Come on now, Alfie," said Stan. "Easy now, boy, that's it, walk nicely now. That's it, come on now. Home soon. Good boy, Alfie."

Hunched and cowed, Alfie trailed miserably behind Stan, halfheartedly trying to stop but giving up when Stan yanked the leash. Too late, he remembered how near he had been to Charlie and home and began barking wildly, making one last lunge to

escape before Stan pulled up the leash so tightly that he was cut off in midbark. He turned his head and gave one last desperate look in the direction of the alleyway before Stan dragged him between the houses on the other side of the clearing.

In the restaurant, Charlie and his mom were sitting at the table with Ken and Rosemary, all just about to start their meal.

"Listen," said Charlie. "I can hear Alfie barking—I'm sure it's him."

"You must have X-ray ears," Ken said, laughing. "I can't hear a thing."

They all fell silent as they strained to listen.

"I can't hear anything either," said Charlie's mom. "Let's have our food before it gets cold. We'll have plenty of time to watch out for him later on."

"But there *was* a dog barking," insisted Charlie. "Couldn't we just check?"

Charlie's mom gave him a stern look. "Later," she said. "Food now, okay?"

"Okay," mumbled Charlie, admitting defeat. "But I'm sure it was him."

CHAPTER TWENTY-THREE

A huge full moon rose behind the trees in Hawkland Woods, lighting up the trees in an unearthly shade of gray blue. Fixit and Sunset emerged from their den for a night out hunting.

Sunset glanced at the hollowed area beneath Alfie's bush. "It's odd without him," she said sadly. "I'd sort of gotten used to the great big lump. I do hope his people were pleased to see him."

"Of course they were," said Fixit. "After all those posters and the way they looked for him, they'll all be going crazy right now. I bet he's forgotten us already!"

Back at the parade of stores, Charlie and his mom were climbing into their car, deeply disappointed once again after a cold vigil at the garbage bins.

"We don't even know if it *was* him at the café," said Charlie's mom.

"I *know* it was," said Charlie. "It *must* have been."

"But the dog they saw didn't have a collar," said Charlie's mom. "If it *was* Alfie, he'd still be wearing his red collar. Perhaps it was just a big scruffy dog that belonged to someone else."

"It *was* him," said Charlie stubbornly. "I *know* it was."

"Well, we can't keep coming here like this!" said Charlie's mom as she put the car into gear and drove off toward their home. "He's only been seen six times in all these months and we don't actually know if it ever *was* Alfie that they saw."

"Six times is a lot, Mom," said Charlie.

"Oh, darling," said Charlie's mom, "I suppose I'm saying we can't go on doing this *forever*, spending every spare moment looking for a dog that we don't even know is still out there. Jenny's offered to buy you a new puppy, so maybe we should think about it."

Charlie didn't say anything. He only rested his head against the cold glass and tried his very best not to cry.

CHAPTER TWENTY-FOUR

"**B**ert!" called Stan. "Look what *I* found!" He let himself into the hallway, dragging Alfie behind him, and slammed the door firmly shut.

Bert came out of the kitchen at the end of the hall and stared in amazement. "Well, blow me down!" he exclaimed. "It's a deerhound, isn't it?"

"Not just *any* deerhound," said Stan. "It's the one off that poster. It *must* be! Look at the state of him! He's been out there for months living rough; you can tell by the smell! Must be the best hunter on the planet to survive that long in the wild—he'll be the perfect dog to take hunting. I can't believe our luck."

They led Alfie into the kitchen, which was surprisingly cozy, despite its untidy state, with two battered armchairs and a very old oven. At one side of the oven, in an alcove with shelves above it, was Lightning, lying in an old dog bed. When he saw Alfie, he half sat up and curled his lip in what was most definitely *not* a smile.

"Lay off, old boy," said Bert. "You have to be nice to the new kid."

Lightning sank down and watched through narrowed eyes as Stan and Bert sat down in the chairs and examined Alfie thoroughly. "What on earth's he been rolling in?" said Bert. "He smells like a fox."

"But look at this chest!" marveled Stan. "Fantastic strength in those shoulders, and his hind legs—strong as a lion—he's *perfect*."

All the time he was talking, Stan kept smoothing Alfie's head. Then he shoved him across to Bert, who started massaging him just below his ears on either side of his neck. This was so pleasant that Alfie's head drooped lower and lower and his front legs buckled.

"That nice, eh?" Bert laughed. "Wow, Stan, he's a pushover, isn't he? Won't take us five minutes to train him."

Bert fetched some blankets and an old coat and made up an extra bed between the chairs, while Stan went back to the shop and bought some more dog food.

To begin with, Alfie couldn't help enjoying all the attention, especially the neck massage and the food, but when he started listening to Stan and Bert's plans he realized with alarm that they wanted to turn him into a hunting dog to take with them to the woods at night. As soon as this dawned on him, he started yelping and running around the room.

Stan grabbed Alfie by the trailing leash and dragged him over to the pile of blankets. "On your bed now," he ordered sternly, pushing Alfie firmly onto his new bed and pressing his back until he collapsed into a miserable heap.

Then the two men turned the main light off, leaving only a table lamp on, and went out of the room.

Lightning let out a low, rumbling growl. "Why don't you go back where you came from," he snarled.

"Don't be angry with me," whined Alfie nervously. "It's not my fault that I'm here. They stole me."

Lightning made a snorting sound. "They only got you 'cause I'm a bit old and I can't walk far these days," he muttered. "My back legs have gone all wobbly, and now they have this new lamp they're dying to try out."

"Lamp?" asked Alfie.

"Birdbrain!" said Lightning rudely. "They're *lampers*—they need a *lamp*—you know, to go *lamping*."

"What *is* lamping?" asked Alfie. "My friends warned me about hunters, but they didn't say anything about *lampers*."

Lightning peered at Alfie. "You really don't know *anything*, do you?" he said.

"I do know *some* things," said Alfie brightly. "I know my boy's name is Charlie and I know beef is my favorite food and I know that I don't go hunting because I promised our cat, Florence."

"Well, you can forget that for a start," said Lightning. "Lamping is a type of hunting. That's why they caught you, so you can help them hunt. They go out in the woods in the early hours and turn on their lamp. It has a fantastic beam and it catches the rabbits or whatever completely unaware, then—this is the fun bit—you get to run down the beam and catch as many rabbits as you can, and Stan and Bert shoot any foxes they see."

Alfie sat with his mouth open, completely stunned.

"They got the new lamp in the mail this morning," Lightning rattled on. "It has a silent switch on it, so the animals aren't alerted by the click, and the beam's so powerful that you can practically see all the way to the moon! I wish my back legs weren't so bad; it's just amazing seeing how many rabbits you can grab in a night."

Alfie curled up in a tight ball, ears flopped right over his eyes, nose covered with one of his paws. "I think I'll rest a little now, if you don't mind," he murmured.

"Suit yourself," said Lightning. "Sweet dreams."

Alfie tossed and turned, trying to think of a way out of the mess he had blundered into.

"Stop fidgeting," growled Lightning. "I can't sleep with all that rustling."

"Sorry," said Alfie. "Suppose I just won't do it, you know, this lamping thing. What would they do?"

"You really *are* a weirdo, aren't you?" said Lightning, attempting to scratch an ear with his stiff back leg and toppling over in the process. "You're a *hound* for goodness' sake—it's what hounds are made for, hunting. It's fun. Just pretend for a while and you'll get used to it. Now be quiet and get some rest."

"*Pretend!*" thought Alfie. "What a good

idea! I can *pretend* that I'll be really good, then they'll let me off the leash and I can escape."

This thought completely calmed him down, and he stretched out on his new bed and enjoyed the softness after the hard floor of his bush den.

CHAPTER TWENTY-FIVE

The first thing Bert and Stan did the next day was wash Alfie in their backyard with the garden hose. He made a terrific fuss, yelping and twirling on the leash, but Stan was very clever at making him behave, alternately shouting angrily, then sounding gentle and kind, until Alfie gave up struggling and stood quaking with cold while Stan picked out all the brambles and twigs and Bert rinsed off the amazing amount of dried mud. Some of the brambles were almost woven into his fur and had to be cut out with scissors.

"Look, Bert," said Stan. "He has some nasty sore places from all those brambles. Hold still, Alfie. We'll fix those for you. There now, isn't that better?"

It *did* feel better, drying out by the warm stove, ointment smeared onto the sore patches that had been very itchy. The only thing he *didn't* like was the lemon smell of the shampoo. He really had loved his foxy perfume.

From the very first day with Bert and Stan, Alfie set out to show them how trustworthy he would be. Every time Stan sat down, Alfie rushed over and laid his head lovingly on Stan's knee and gave him a paw, and when Stan was looking at the newspaper Alfie nudged his nose charmingly underneath it and gave Stan a huge, messy lick.

"Get off!" Stan laughed.

"He's really taken to you, that dog," said Bert. "Look how he follows you around."

"Probably 'cause it was me who found him," said Stan. "He's the devoted type; hounds are like that. It won't be long before we can take him out with us and give him a try. Doesn't bark much either—have you noticed? Only yelped a bit when we were washing him. They don't bark much, deer-hounds—just perfect for lamping."

CHAPTER TWENTY-SIX

They chose a moonless night for Alfie's first lamping session. Alfie, still on the leash, walked perfectly to heel as they set off out of the house for the first time since Stan had grabbed him. Weeks of pretending to be the most obedient dog in the world had paid off. But, to Alfie's dismay, Bert was carrying a shotgun as well as the silent-switch lamp. Alfie hadn't realized that they might bring anything as nasty as a gun.

"I can't believe how easy it's been to train him," said Stan as they left the outskirts of

the woods and plunged into the undergrowth, away from the houses and deep
into the heart of the rough woodland.
"He just follows me everywhere—even lies
outside the bathroom when I'm in there!
Old Lightning was never as eager to please
as this young fella."

Alfie nosed his snout into Stan's hand.

"Good boy," said Stan. "Quiet now. Not
a sound."

They walked for half an hour, deeper
and deeper into the thickest areas of bush
and brambles, through narrow pathways,
some of which Alfie recognized from his
nighttime travels. Abruptly, Stan gave the
leash a sharp tug and they all stopped. It
was so dark that you could only just make
out the tops of the trees against the night
sky. No one moved for several minutes. Alfie
waited, wondering if they were going to
walk on again when suddenly, noiselessly,
Bert turned on the lamp.

To Alfie's utter horror, the brilliant beam of light revealed the worst sight in the world: Fixit, caught in the devastating glare, transfixed with shock.

Stan let go of Alfie's leash and raised his gun. In a split second, Alfie hurled himself at Bert, knocking the lamp to the ground, where it rolled around crazily, lighting up Bert's feet and Stan's angry face.

"Run, Fixit!" barked Alfie. "Run for your life. They have a gun!"

Total pandemonium broke loose. Two shots rang out, then someone picked up the lamp and Alfie heard the furious voices of the two men yelling his name. Alfie raced into the woodland as fast as he could. He ran on and on, twisting and turning to avoid the beam of light, ripping himself on brambles, catching his flailing leash on branches, stopping to yank himself free, then plunging on through woven walls of undergrowth.

At last, he left the voices and the light far behind and stopped to catch his breath. One of his back legs was feeling really painful and he started whimpering with fright. Alfie waited, crouched in a dense patch of bracken, and listened, his deerhound ears going through all the different earstyles as he strained to make completely sure that he had lost them.

There was no sound, so he laid his nose on his paws and decided to wait for a good chunk of time until he was sure they hadn't been able to track him down.

CHAPTER TWENTY-SEVEN

Fixit dived headfirst into the den and landed on top of Sunset in a shower of earth.

"Watch out!" she said. "Hey, what's the matter? Did something happen?"

Fixit lay alongside her, panting. "Hunters!" he managed to gasp. "They had a gun—and, even worse, they had Alfie."

"*Alfie?*" exclaimed Sunset. "But he went home *ages* ago. Are you sure it was him?"

"He saved me," said Fixit. "Knocked the lamp clean out of the man's hands. It was definitely him."

They lay in the darkness, straining their ears and noses for any sign that Fixit had been followed. After a while, they began to relax.

"They were miles away from here," said Fixit. "I don't think it's very likely that they'd find us. Anyway, I came home the long way, to put them off the scent."

"Did they have any other dogs—any terriers?" asked Sunset.

"No," said Fixit. "Only Alfie, so I think we're safe."

At that very moment, they heard a rustling and scratching outside the entrance to their den. The two foxes huddled together, terrified.

Then came the voice they knew so well.

"It's only me. It's all right—I waited till they were gone and came the long way. I'd never bring them here. It's me—Alfie."

Fixit and Sunset scrambled out and found Alfie collapsed in front of his bush lair.

"What on earth were you doing with those horrible men?" asked Fixit. "We thought you were safe at home *ages* ago."

Alfie let out a low half howl. "So sorry!" he whimpered. "*So* sorry, but my back leg hurts. It really, *really* hurts. I think I must have caught it on something."

"Let's have a sniff," said Sunset, waffling

her nose up and down Alfie's back legs as he lay trying to stifle yelps. "He's been shot," she whispered to Fixit. "Take a sniff—you can smell the gunpowder and the blood."

"I'm sorry." Alfie kept apologizing. "It wasn't my fault, honestly. They kidnapped me so they could train me as a lamper's dog. The only way I could get them to trust me was to pretend that I was happy to do it— AARF!" He gave a loud yelp as his wounded back leg gave a sharp twinge. "What's wrong? Why does my leg hurt so much?"

"Now then, dear," said Sunset, trying to sound in charge, "you shouldn't panic, but it smells as if you were shot."

Alfie panicked.

He tried to scramble to his feet, yelping and barking, but crashed down into the bushes as all his legs gave way with sheer terror.

"Stop!" barked Fixit. "You *must* keep quiet or they'll come back and find us."

Alfie clamped his teeth together.

"Can you shuffle under your bush, Alfie?" asked Fixit. "You'll need shelter in case it rains."

"Couldn't I just stay here?" asked Alfie. "I don't want to move right now."

In the end, when they saw that he really was too weak and exhausted to move, Fixit and Sunset lay down on either side of Alfie to keep him warm.

"Sorry I smell so awful," he said. "They washed me with some lemon stuff. I hope you don't mind."

"It *is* a bit smelly," agreed Sunset. "But never mind. You can roll in our nice messy patch tomorrow. We'll soon have you smelling like a fox again."

CHAPTER TWENTY-EIGHT

It was a Sunday morning. Charlie and his mom sat miserably at the breakfast table, their toast growing cold in front of them.

"I don't *want* another puppy," said Charlie. "It's very nice of Jenny to offer, but I still think we can find Alfie. How could we have another dog and have fun with it when Alfie's still out there in the woods?"

"No one's seen him at *all* since that day at the café," said his mom, "and we really *don't* know if it ever *was* him."

"Can't we go and put up some more posters?" asked Charlie. "Just *one* more bunch. The others have either blown away or gotten ratty in the wind. Please. We could go today; we're not doing anything."

Charlie's mom let out a huge sigh. "All right," she said. "Just *one* more bunch and *one* more look, then that's it, Charlie. You just have to face it. He isn't coming back. It's sad, it's awful, but the miracle just isn't going to happen."

Charlie left his toast and went to pull on his coat and his lucky light-up sneakers. While his mom was getting ready, he hurried outside and leaned over the front gate.

He hadn't sent his magic thought waves out for weeks, what with school and the cold weather. Now he fixed his eyes on the end of the road, where he had watched Jenny's van drive Alfie away all those months ago, and sent a tsunami, full of more than hope, full of absolute belief that Alfie would be there this one last time.

"Ready, darling?" called his mom.

"Yes, Mom," said Charlie. "I'm out here, ready and waiting. Let's go."

A gray dawn had broken on the strange little group huddled outside the foxes' den. Alfie was in a bad state, whimpering and panting. Sunset got up and examined Alfie's damaged leg, stretched out in the gloom. It was covered in dried blood, with a cluster of dark holes right in the center of the top part.

"How does it feel, Alf?" asked Fixit, nudging Alfie awake. "It's stopped bleeding, so *that's* a good thing."

"Hurts," whined Alfie. "Hurts worse—am I going to die?"

"Of *course* not," soothed Sunset. "We'll work out what to do, won't we, Fixit?"

"Definitely," agreed Fixit, though he didn't have the faintest idea what on earth they could do to help. "First of all, I'll go for a quick scavenge and fetch us some breakfast."

"Don't go yet," said Sunset, feeling a bit

jittery about being left alone with the anxious invalid. "I'm not very hungry anyway."

"Neither am I," said Alfie miserably. "And I'm *always* hungry. I'm going to die, aren't I? You just don't want to tell me."

He let out a volley of yelps.

"Shhh!" said Sunset. "I *promise* you're not going to die, all right? I *know* about these things."

"Do you?" asked Alfie, brightening up.

"Yes, I do," replied Sunset firmly. "Now just lie still while we think up our plan of action."

Sunset and Fixit wandered to the edge of the narrow pathway in the undergrowth, which they had hollowed out as they made their way to and from their den each day.

"He's in really bad shape," said Sunset. "We can't just leave him here. His leg won't heal up on its own. What *are* we going to do?"

"For once," said Fixit, "I really have no idea whatsoever."

They sat down, leaning against each other, watching the morning light grow stronger. After a while, they glanced back at Alfie, who had slipped into a light sleep, making little yipping noises.

"I'll go and find us some food," said Fixit. "I'll try to make a plan while I'm looking."

He bustled off through the bushes and Sunset went back to Alfie. She stretched herself out along his back to keep him warm.

"Don't leave me," murmured Alfie.

"Of course not," said Sunset.

Charlie and his mom arrived at the woods and systematically repostered as much of the area as they could. They had made some new posters on their computer, with an extra part saying that Alfie would look older and scruffier by now and offering a reward.

"We should have offered a reward the first time," said Charlie.

"I know," said his mom. "We were in such a hurry to print them that I wasn't thinking straight. I'm sorry."

It took them two hours to tack every single new poster to trees and fence posts and they finally sat down on a bench in a picnic area to rest. "I'll just put up the last one on this bulletin board here," said Charlie's mom. "Then we're done."

Lurking underneath the picnic table, Fixit froze and waited until Charlie's mom pushed the tacks into the last poster and went to sit with Charlie, their backs conveniently turned to the table.

"I'm so tired," said Charlie's mom. "Let's sit here for a bit."

"Okay," said Charlie.

"At least we tried our best," said his mom.

"Our very, *very* best in the world," agreed Charlie.

Fixit flattened himself and slunk away into the bushes with no sound at all, like a spirit of the woods.

"They're here!" barked Fixit, crashing back through the pathway to the den.

"Who?" asked Sunset, jumping up in alarm. "The horrible men?"

"No, no!" Fixit laughed. "Alfie's people! They're at the picnic place—just around the corner from here. They can come and help him."

"How?" asked Sunset. "Look at him."

Fixit looked. Alfie had gotten worse even in the short time that Fixit had been away. He was breathing in short gasps, his eyes half open, whimpering to himself. "Come on, Alf," said Fixit, lying next to Alfie and giving his face a lick. "Your people are *so* nearby. Can you get up and hobble a bit? They're *so* close."

Alfie rolled his eyes toward his friend and groaned, then slid back into sleep.

"This is *awful*," said Fixit desperately. "They won't be there for long. How on earth can we let them know he's here?"

Sunset jumped up. "*I* know," she said. "I know *just* what to do. Follow me."

CHAPTER TWENTY-NINE

"**W**ell, my love," said Charlie's mom, "we can't sit here for the rest of our lives. We'd better be getting home—oh, look, Charlie." She lowered her voice to a whisper. "There are two foxes over there on the edge of the clearing. Don't make a sound or they'll run off."

Charlie and his mom sat perfectly still, watching the pair of foxes, expecting them to slink hastily into the undergrowth, but they just stood there.

"They're looking at us, Mom," whispered Charlie, not moving a muscle. "And one of them's carrying something."

Very cautiously, one slow-motion step at a time, poised for instant flight, Fixit and Sunset inched their way across the open ground until they were so close that Charlie could have reached out and touched them. Then they stopped and Fixit stepped forward and laid something on the ground at their feet.

It was Alfie's broken collar.

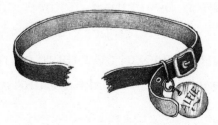

Charlie's mouth dropped open as he recognized it. "Mom!" he breathed. "It's Alfie's collar." Very slowly, Charlie bent down and picked it up, but as soon as he moved Sunset and Fixit turned and fled back to the far edge of the clearing, where they stood watching with unblinking amber eyes.

"Look, Mom!" said Charlie. "It has his name tag! They've brought us his collar. They must know where he is!"

"But they're *foxes*!" said Charlie's mom. "How could they know *anything*?"

"*I* don't know," said Charlie. "But they brought us his collar, didn't they?"

"Let's see if they let us follow them," said Charlie's mom, her heart hammering with shocked astonishment. "*Very* slowly, so we don't frighten them."

As soon as Charlie and his mom got up, Sunset and Fixit trotted off in front of them for a few paces, then stopped and turned to

make sure they were being followed. Charlie and his mom stopped too, then the two foxes set off again, Charlie and his mom hurrying along behind them, stopping when they

stopped and following when they set off again. They went on like this, stopping and starting, until the woods got thicker and more hidden from the usual pathways and clear areas.

"It's getting too overgrown to get through," said Charlie's mom, dragging aside huge tangles of bramble that clutched at their clothing like squid tentacles.

Suddenly, they rounded a corner in the tunnel-like pathway through the undergrowth and stopped.

Alfie lay directly in front of them, on his side, very still, a green rope leash around his neck looped underneath him, the wounded leg matted with dried blood.

Sunset and Fixit stood farther away at the mouth of their den, watching.

"*Alfie!*" yelled Charlie. He flung himself down in the mud and gently smoothed Alfie's face. "Look, Mom! It's *him*! We've found him! It's okay, Alf, you're okay now. We've got you, we've got you."

Charlie's mom knelt down and examined the leg. "This looks bad, Charlie," she said. "I think someone shot him."

"*Shot* him!" gasped Charlie. "But he *will* be all right, Mom, won't he, now that we found him?"

"Yes, darling," said his mom. "I'm sure he'll be fine—I'll call Jenny and Rita and the vet and see if they can come find us and help carry him out. The vet can bring one of those big stretchers they use."

Charlie sat next to Alfie, smoothing his fur and crying all over him. "We found him!" He laughed through his tears. "We actually found him—I *told* you, didn't I? I knew he was still here."

"It was your magic thought waves that did it," said his mom, smiling, as she dialed Jenny's number with trembling fingers. "Jenny? You'll never guess what—we found him."

Fixit and Sunset watched as Jenny and Rita arrived, bringing the vet and one of the veterinary nurses. They bundled Alfie onto a large plastic stretcher and strapped him on securely.

"I wish he were conscious," said Sunset. "I would've liked to have said good-bye."

"Me too," said Fixit. "Still, at least we *know* he's made it back to his people this time. At least we *know* he's safe."

Charlie looked back and caught their eye as the group of rescuers started shuffling their way out of the thicket.

"Thank you," he called to them, but the two foxes turned and disappeared into the shadowy mouth of their den.

"Well, my dear," said Fixit. "We'll have to move out of here right now after all these people have seen where we live."

"Pity," said Sunset. "It was such a nice little hideaway. But you're right, of course, and I suppose it *could* have been a teensy bit bigger. Won't be long till spring and there'll be cubs to think about."

"Come on, then," said Fixit. "I saw a nice place around the back of the café, right in the middle of a dip full of brambles. No one'll ever find us there—especially not any huge lost dogs!"

CHAPTER THIRTY

A lfie woke up and thought he must be dreaming. He had dreamed of being home so often, but this time it seemed absolutely real. It *was* real. He was lying on his beanbag in the kitchen, his back leg heavily bandaged, and Charlie was sitting next to him, gently stroking his head.

"Look, Mom," said Charlie, "he's waking up. Hey, Alfie, it's me. You're back home."

Charlie's mom bent down to ruffle Alfie's fur. "Look at *you*," she said, smiling. "What a scare you gave us, you naughty boy."

"It wasn't *his* fault, Mom," said Charlie. "Was it, Alf? I wish he could talk and tell us all his adventures, especially about the foxes. Deerhounds are supposed to *hate* foxes! Who *were* they, Alf? How did they know what to do?"

Alfie raised his head and slapped his great wet tongue across his master's face.

Florence jumped down from the counter and landed with a thump on the beanbag. "So you came back to us," she purred.

Alfie looked at her and smiled. "I kept my promise," he said. "I never chased anything, not even a mouse."

"Move over, then," said Florence, "and you can tell me all about it."

"Later," said Alfie, as his eyelids drooped and he began to doze off again. "Right now, I want to go back to sleep—so I can wake up again and find I'm still here. I'm just *so* happy. It's *wonderful* to be home."